THE
CALICO CAT
Cafe

Narinder Dhami

Illustrated by **Jemma Jamie Skidmore**

OXFORD
UNIVERSITY PRESS

I grew up in a community exactly like Ravina's. My family lived on an estate too, and I had a very diverse group of friends. Some were Indian, like my dad, some  were Black and my very best friend was Italian.

Just like in the story, people who lived on the estate used to help each other whenever they could. We had shops on our estate too, just like Ravina. But we didn't have a cafe, and we didn't have a community centre, either. We were lucky though, because there was a park close by where we could roller-skate and ride our bikes!

Finally, I'm very pleased that there's a cat in this story because I have five of my own! I've never owned a calico cat though. Maybe that should be cat number six?

Narinder Dhami

Chapter 1
Mystery at the Cafe

Mollie Carter and her friends were waiting for me when I walked out of school. I knew they would be, because our teacher, Mr Sharma, had said I was a brilliant reader. He'd called me the 'class bookworm'.

'Oh, look. It's Ravina the bookworm,' Mollie said. 'Or maybe she's just a *worm*.'

Her friends giggled. I couldn't say a word. It was like my tongue was tied up in knots.

'Worms are quiet and dull and boring,' Mollie said. 'No one ever really notices them.' She grinned. 'Just like Ravina.'

I walked faster to get away from her. Mollie Carter was so cool and confident. Not like me. I didn't understand why Mollie picked on me sometimes, just because I was quiet and I loved books.

I could think of loads of smart things to say to Mollie, but only when I was alone in my bedroom. Never when we were at school.

My brother Jeet was outside the gates
looking for me. For once, I was really glad to
see him. Believe me, *that* doesn't happen very
often. We fight a lot, but he's all right really.

'Can we stop at Mrs Mac's cafe to buy cola?'
I asked Jeet. The big housing estate where we
lived was only a few minutes' walk away.

Jeet groaned. 'Not that strange old cafe,
Ravina! It smells weird.'

'The cola tastes the same though, wherever we buy it,' I shot back. I knew he really wanted to go to the burger place next door instead.

'You've got a smart answer for everything, Ravina,' Jeet said with a grin. But it was easier talking back to him than to Mollie. I *have* to stand up for myself at home, with three older brothers trying to boss me around.

In the middle of the estate there was a row of shops. Some of them were empty and boarded up. The community centre was there, too, but it had been closed down by the council last year to save money. It was a real shame. There had been so much going on there every day. I used to go to a children's book group and a homework club. I was really upset when it closed.

Mrs Mac's cafe was next door to the burger bar, but it didn't have bright lights, a flashing sign or music playing. The windows were covered with old-fashioned net curtains. The green sign above the door had *Mrs Mac's Cafe* painted in gold letters, but the paint was peeling off. Inside, it was a bit shabby too. The tables and chairs were old and wobbly, and the walls needed painting. But I didn't care. I liked it that way.

Mrs Mac was a friend of my mum's. That was why I was allowed to go to the cafe to do my homework sometimes. Our house was always noisy and crammed with people, so I loved the peace and quiet of the cafe. Like me, Mrs Mac was a bookworm, and we always had something to talk about.

When Jeet and I went into the cafe, there was no one inside except Mrs Mac. She was the smiliest person I knew, and she was always cracking jokes. But today she looked worried.

'Hello,' she called, but she didn't come over and chat to me like she usually did.

Jeet went to the fridge to get the cola, and I took my new library book out of my bag. I wanted to show it to Mrs Mac but she didn't look up from the letter she was reading.

'Ravina, put that book away.' Jeet rolled his eyes as he paid Mrs Mac. 'You're not at school now!'

'Bye, Mrs Mac,' I called as we left.

But Mrs Mac didn't reply. It was like she didn't even hear me.

Outside the cafe, we bumped into my mum. She was on her way to her second job, cleaning offices in town.

'Everything all right, you two?' Mum asked.

For a moment, I thought of telling Mum about Mollie. But she looked so tired, I decided to wait.

'Fine,' I said. 'But is Mrs Mac OK, Mum?'

Mum looked surprised. 'As far as I know. I'll see you later.'

I couldn't help wondering about Mrs Mac though. It was a bit of a mystery.

Chapter 2
A Shock for Ravina

Every morning was like rush hour in our house. My mum, my brothers and me were all trying to shower, get dressed, eat breakfast and leave for work, school or college on time.

Manny and Sham were arguing about whose turn it was to use the bathroom. Jeet was eating cereal and playing a noisy game on his phone. Mum was trying to fix the broken toaster.

My gran and grandad were watching TV with the sound turned right up. I was reading my library book with my hands over my ears.

Dad arrived home, yawning after his night shift. 'Morning, everyone,' he said, tweaking my ponytail. 'Looking forward to the school holidays, Ravina?'

I nodded eagerly. Today was our last day at school for two weeks. 'Yes, Dad,' I replied, 'I'm going to—'

'Read hundreds of books!' Jeet interrupted. I pulled a face at him, but he was dead right. Best of all, I wouldn't have to see Mollie Carter in the holidays, either.

Jeet and I were five minutes late leaving for school, so we had to hurry. We were almost there when Jeet spotted his friend Leo up ahead. He sprinted off to join him and left me on my own. I slowed down a bit. There were still two minutes before the bell. I'd make it easily.

Someone came up behind me.

'Hello, Worm,' said Mollie.

I didn't turn around.

'Hey, I'm talking to you, Worm!' Mollie said. She came up alongside me, and I backed away from her, towards someone's garden fence. There was a nail sticking out of one of the fence panels, but I didn't notice it. Not until I heard a loud tearing sound.

Horrified, I stared down at my blue school sweatshirt. One of the sleeves had caught on the nail. There was a long, jagged rip in it.

'Oops!' said Mollie, her eyes wide. 'You should be more careful.' She ran off into school.

Tears filled my eyes as I looked down at my torn sweatshirt. I felt terrible. How would I tell my parents I needed a new one?

There was never enough money to go around,
even though my mum and dad worked
really hard.

Then I heard the school bell ring. So
now I was late too. This was all Mollie
Carter's fault.

* * *

I shouldn't have done it. It was just too easy though.

I was first into the classroom after break, and there was Mollie's homework sitting on top of her open bag. Quick as a flash, I grabbed the sheets of paper and stuffed them behind the radiator.

'Where's my homework?' Mollie asked when she came in. I sat watching as she hunted around for it. I said nothing as Mollie became more and more flustered.

Mr Sharma was annoyed. 'You can do it again during the holidays, Mollie,' he snapped. 'Maybe I should give you some extra work, too!'

Serves you right, Mollie Carter, I thought. But I didn't feel pleased that Mollie had got into trouble. I felt a bit mean ...

After school, I met Jeet at the gates.

'Yay! Holidays!' Jeet yelled happily, swinging his bag around. 'It's going to be brilliant, Ravina!'

'Yes,' I agreed. I wasn't excited though. I felt very flat and really down. Secretly, I knew it was because I'd been mean to Mollie Carter. I just didn't want to admit it.

Jeet wanted to stop at the burger bar on the way home. So I decided to pop into the cafe and see Mrs Mac. I was sure she was worrying about something.

I left Jeet buying chips and went next door to the cafe. There was a large sign in the window. It said "CLOSING DOWN".

Chapter 3
A Helping Hand

'The new owners of the building have told me the rent's going up, Ravina,' Mrs Mac said sadly. There were tears in her eyes. 'I just can't afford it. I have to close.'

I felt like crying myself. Today had gone from bad to worse. I couldn't imagine life without Mrs Mac and her cafe. I spent so much time there, especially since the community centre had closed. It was my quiet place when I needed to get away from the noise and bustle of home. I also knew that a lot of older people who lived on the estate liked popping into the cafe for a cup of tea and a slice of cake. They'd miss it, too.

'There must be something we can do,'
I said.

Mrs Mac and I were sitting at one of the
tables in the window. Outside, I noticed
a pretty little cat lying on the steps of the
old community centre. She was white with
patches of black and ginger. I watched the cat
as she rolled around in the sunshine.

Then an idea suddenly crept into my head.

'Mrs Mac,' I said, 'You know how there was always something going on at the community centre? Remember I was in the kids' book group and the homework club?'

Mrs Mac looked surprised. 'Oh, yes, it was a wonderful place, Ravina,' she agreed. 'I used to go to a book group there, myself. And the writers' group too. It was a real meeting place for all kinds of people, wasn't it? Mums and babies. Elderly people.'

'Jeet was in a coding club, Sham used to go to the art class and my grandparents went to the community centre to meet their friends.' I was so excited, the words just came tumbling out of me. 'Mrs Mac, why can't *your* cafe be the new community centre?'

'What?' Mrs Mac stared at me in shock.

'People could meet here like they used to at the community centre,' I explained, glancing around the large cafe. 'There's plenty of room for clubs and classes, and you'd get lots of new customers, so you could afford to stay open.'

'Ravina, that's a brilliant idea,' Mrs Mac said slowly. 'There's just one problem ... '

'What's that?' I asked.

'I'd have to renovate the cafe first,' Mrs Mac replied. 'I've been putting it off for ages because of the cost—'

'I'll help you with the painting!' I broke in. 'How hard can it be?'

Mrs Mac laughed. 'Well, I can afford a few tins of paint,' she said. 'Are you sure you want to help, Ravina?'

'Yes, I do!' I replied eagerly.

* * *

The next morning, I put on some old clothes. I'd already told my mum I was helping Mrs Mac paint the cafe, and she'd said she would come too. I'd also shown my mum the rip in my sweatshirt. I didn't say anything about Mollie, though.

'Never mind, love,' Mum said. 'Accidents happen. It was getting a bit small for you now, anyway.' So then I felt a bit better.

'What's going on?' asked Dad, noticing the old clothes Mum and I were wearing. My three brothers and Gran and Grandad were staring at us, too.

'We're helping Mrs Mac renovate the cafe,' I explained. 'It's going to be the new community centre.'

'It was Ravina's idea,' Mum added. Everyone stared at me even harder.

'What?' I said, feeling uncomfortable.

'Where's my *real* sister gone? Quiet little Ravina the bookworm?' Manny teased. I pulled a face at him.

When Mum and I arrived at the cafe, I started to worry. I'd suddenly realized how *big* the place was. I was glad Mum was there, but there was still a lot of work, even with three of us.

'Let's have a cup of tea first,' said Mrs Mac.

We were drinking our tea when the door opened. In trooped Dad, Grandad, Manny, Sham and Jeet. They were all wearing old clothes too, and Dad was carrying a stepladder.

'Thought you might need some help,' Sham said.

'Your gran's making lunch, and she'll bring it over later,' Grandad added.

I grinned. 'Let's get started then!' I said.

Chapter 4
Many Hands Make Light Work

While we were moving the furniture, some of my parents' friends popped in to see what was going on. They stayed to help. Before long, we had quite a crowd of people.

Mrs Mac had bought some pale green paint for the walls. Mum, Mrs Mac and I washed the walls down, and then we started painting.

'I can repair your shop sign, Mrs Mac,' Sham said, 'and I could also paint a mural on that long wall next to the counter, if you like?'

'What do you think, Ravina?' Mrs Mac asked.

'Great idea!' I said eagerly. Sham was good at art. He was studying it at college.

'I'll pop home and get my paints,' said Sham.

The door opened. It was Jeet's friend Leo
and his dad, Mr Thomas. Mr Thomas was
carrying his toolbox.

'Hey, Ravina,' Leo said. 'Jeet messaged me,
and my dad wondered if he could help. He's
a carpenter.'

I turned to Mrs Mac. 'Maybe Mr Thomas
could fix the wobbly tables and chairs?' I
suggested. Mrs Mac nodded.

'I'll have a go,' Mr Thomas said, and opened his toolbox. 'This is a great idea of yours, Ravina. We all miss the community centre.'

'You can help too, Leo,' Jeet laughed, passing him a clean paintbrush.

By the time Sham came back with his paints, a couple more of my mum's friends had also stopped by.

'Look what I found!' Sham said. The little cat I'd seen yesterday had followed him into the cafe. She came over and rubbed against my legs. I wanted to stroke her, but I had paint on my hands.

Meanwhile, my mum's friends were looking around.

'This place needs new curtains, tablecloths and cushions for the chairs,' said Aunty Rita. 'Remember how lovely and bright the community centre was?'

'I'm not sure I can afford that,' Mrs Mac said anxiously.

'What about making them out of patchwork?' my mum suggested. 'Then we can use bits of different material. I'm sure people on the estate will donate whatever they can.'

'Mrs Mac, don't you think the furniture would look much nicer if we painted it?' I said thoughtfully, as Mr Thomas fixed a wobbly chair leg. 'Maybe people would donate leftover paint, too?'

'That sounds wonderful!' Mrs Mac replied.

'I'll make some posters asking for donations,' said Manny. 'We can put them up around the estate.'

I could hardly believe how fast we were getting on, with so many people helping. Then Gran and a couple of her friends arrived with piles of sandwiches, cakes and freshly-made samosas.

'I've had an idea, Mrs Mac,' said Gran, handing out sandwiches. 'Why don't we have a bake sale to raise money? Then you can buy new cups and saucers and plates.'

'Thanks, that's a good idea,' Mrs Mac said gratefully. I smiled and slipped the cat a bit of chicken.

Over the next few days, more people from the estate came to help. I was shy at first because I didn't know some of them very well. But Mrs Mac kept telling everyone this had been my idea, and they all wanted to talk to me. They kept telling me how much they loved the cafe becoming the new community centre, and how clever I was to think of it. So after a while, I forgot to be shy. There was too much going on.

We had plenty of leftover paint and material that people had donated. Mr Thomas had fixed the tables and chairs, and people were painting them different colours. Our neighbour, Mrs Nowak, offered to paint the furniture with pretty flowers and birds.

'This is traditional Polish folk art,' she said, showing me and Mrs Mac pictures on her phone. We loved it!

Meanwhile, Sham was working on the mural. It was a painting of the estate, with the cafe in the middle.

* * *

'I think I might change the name of the cafe, Ravina,' Mrs Mac said a week later.

'What will you call it?' I asked. We were watching Sham sketch our house on the mural. I was holding the cat, who visited us every day. She lay in my arms like a baby, purring loudly. We still didn't know whose cat she was, but she didn't look like a stray.

The cafe was still busy with helpers. A few parents were organizing the special corner for babies and toddlers. People had donated toys and books. Mrs Nowak was painting flowers on the furniture. Aunty Rita was wobbling on top of a stepladder. She was hanging the first pair of new patchwork curtains. They were stripy, spotty and floral and all different colours.

'I don't know yet,' Mrs Mac said. 'Don't the curtains look great?'

I nodded. 'You look like you're made of patchwork too,' I told the cat. 'You're all different colours.'

'These white, black and ginger cats are called *calico cats*,' Mrs Mac explained. Then she and I stared at each other with excitement.

'*The Calico Cat Cafe!*' we said together.

Chapter 5
A New Beginning

By the end of the school holidays, *The Calico Cat Cafe* was finished. Everyone who'd helped met up at the cafe for the grand reopening.

The cafe looked completely different, inside and out. Sham had repainted the sign, and he'd added a picture of the calico cat. She was also part of the mural, sitting outside the cafe.

All the walls and the furniture had been painted. The cafe was now bright, clean and modern. The patchwork curtains, cushions and tablecloths looked amazing.

Gran's bake sale had been a huge success. It had raised enough money for Mrs Mac to buy new crockery and cutlery. Best of all, the local newspaper had heard about what we were doing. They were sending a reporter and a photographer to interview Mrs Mac and me, and take pictures.

'You'll be famous, Ravina!' Jeet teased. I laughed. I wasn't even nervous, like I would have been a little while ago. I just wanted the cafe to be a big success.

I helped Mrs Mac hand out tea and cake while we waited for the newspaper people. When I saw the calico cat outside the door, I rushed to let her in. I was sure the photographer would want to take her photo too.

As I finished my lemon cake, I saw someone I knew. Mollie Carter and her mum were outside the cafe. Whenever I saw Mollie, my heart used to sink. This time, it didn't.

Mollie and her mum were taping something to the lamp post. I was curious and went over to the window to look. It was a poster. At the top, it said "LOST", and underneath was a photo of a calico cat.

I flung the door open. 'Mollie!' I called.

Mollie spun around. She looked shocked when she saw me.

'I think your cat might be in here,' I explained, opening the door wider. The calico cat ran over to me, and Mollie saw her. She immediately burst into tears.

'Marigold!' Mollie sobbed. 'I missed you so much!' She scooped the cat up into her arms and gave her a big hug. Marigold began to purr.

'Oh, thank goodness!' said Ms Carter, looking very relieved. 'She's been missing for so long. Say thank you to Ravina, Mollie.'

'Thank you,' Mollie whispered.

'We've been feeding her,' I explained. 'And Mrs Mac's named the cafe after her. Look!' I gestured at the sign. 'Why don't you come in?'

I led Mollie and her mum into the cafe.
Mrs Mac gave Ms Carter a cup of tea, and I
showed Mollie the mural with the picture of
Marigold. She looked thrilled.

'I'm sorry I was mean to you,' Mollie said
suddenly.

'I'm sorry I was mean to *you*,' I replied.
Mollie looked puzzled.

'It was me who hid your homework,'
I confessed.

'Well, I was mean to you first,' Mollie said. She sighed. 'It's just – I wish I was a good reader like you, Ravina. My mum's always trying to make me read more!'

'I can show you some of my favourite books if you like?' I offered eagerly.

'I'd love that,' Mollie replied, brightening up.

'Ravina, the reporter's here,' said Mrs Mac. She was leading a woman with a notebook and a man with a camera towards me. The reporter smiled when she saw Marigold in Mollie's arms.

'Is this the cat that inspired the cafe's new name?' she asked.

'Yes, this is Marigold,' I replied.

'And are you two girls friends?' the reporter added, writing in her notebook.

Mollie and I glanced at each other. 'Yes!' we both said, and we smiled.